W9-DDC-900

Ma, I'm a Farmer

To Fred, Ann, and Jennifer ("Goldie")

—M.M.

Ma, I'm a Farmer

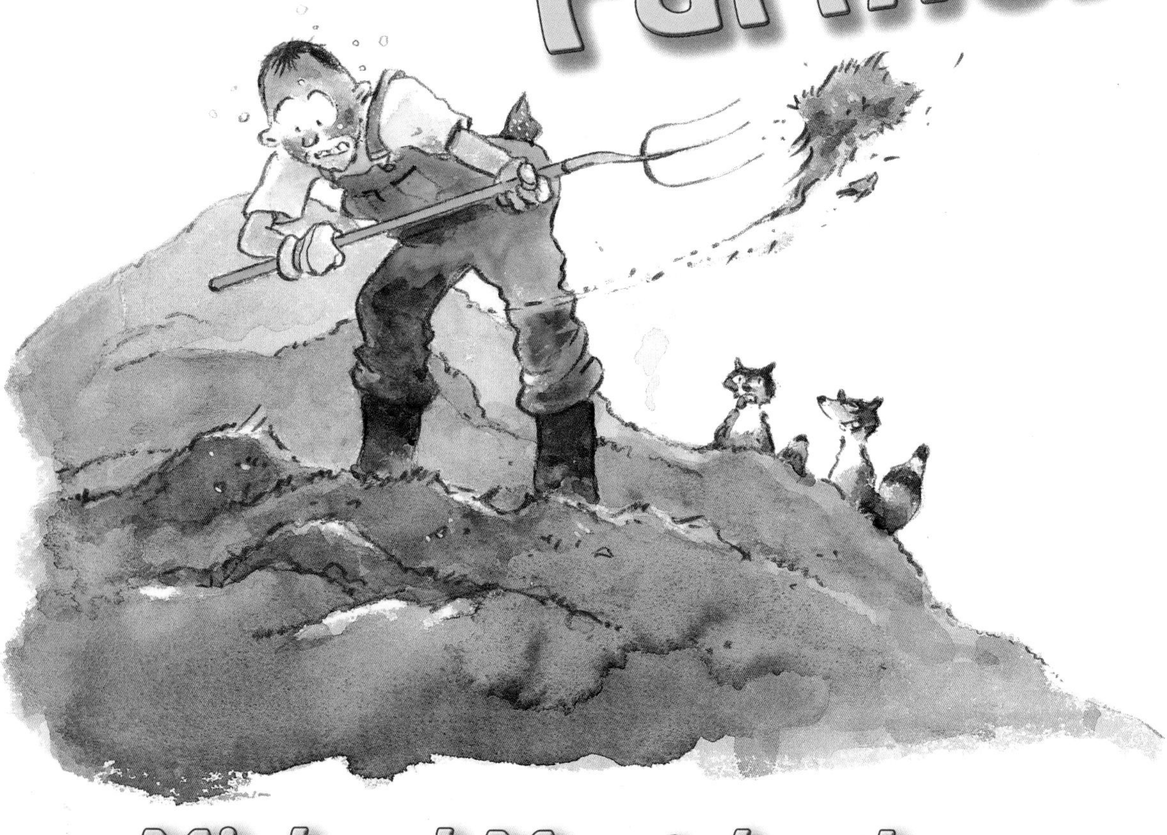

Michael Martchenko

Annick Press Ltd. • Toronto • New York • Vancouver

Fred was a computer operator.

He worked for a very large company in a very large city. Every morning, Fred would put his lunch in his briefcase, say goodbye to his cat Annie and his goldfish Jennifer, and rush to catch the downtown bus.

One morning Fred thought, "I'm tired of the city, I'm tired of the traffic and the pollution, and I'm really tired of staring at that computer all day... It's boring, and it's making my eyes go square."

That night Fred thought and thought. "I know," he finally said. "That's what I'm going to do!"

He picked up the phone and called his mother.

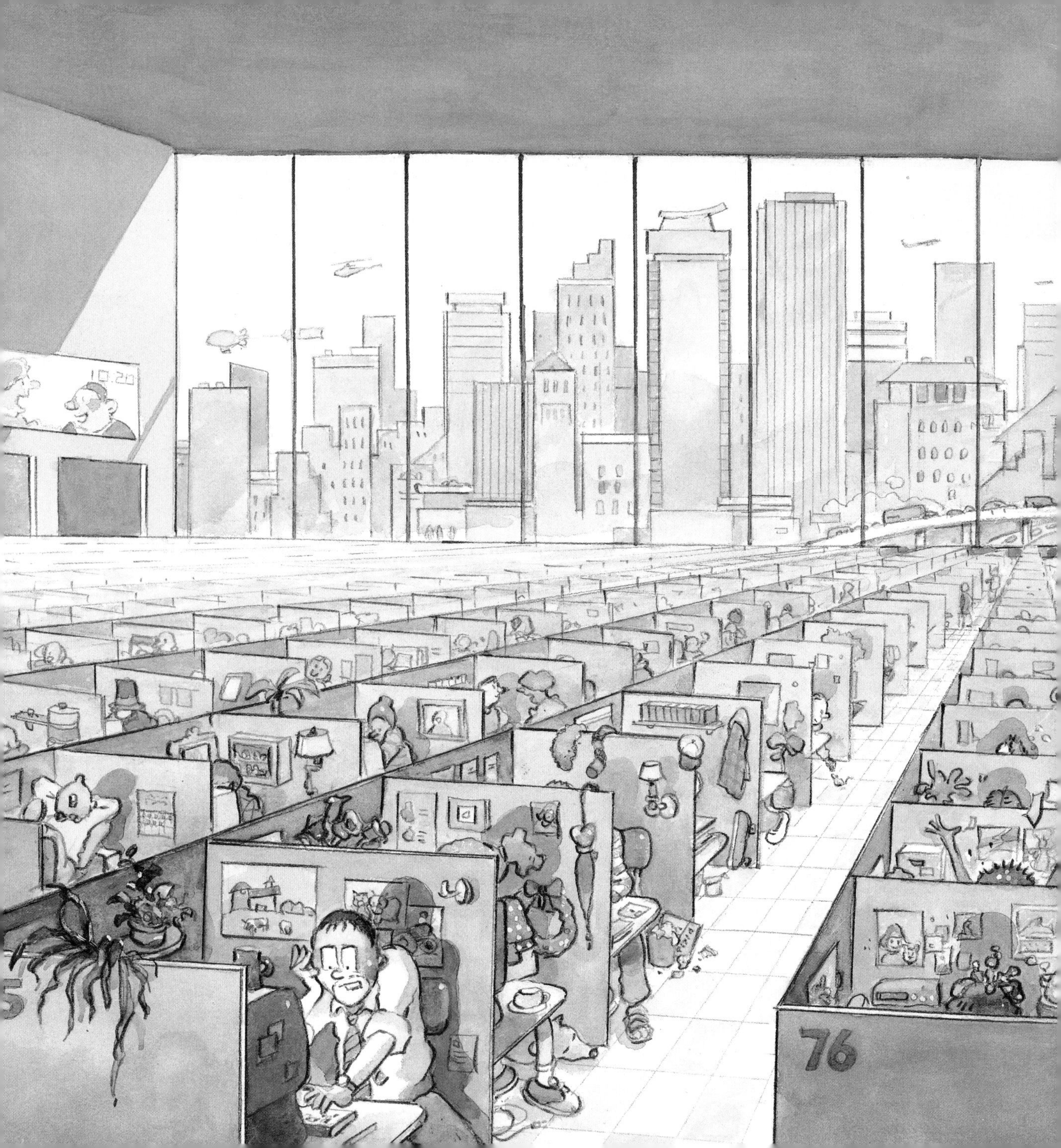
10:20
76

"Ma, I'm a farmer!" said Fred. "I mean, I'm going to be a farmer. I'm going to buy a farm with lots of space."

"That's nice, dear," said his mom, "but watch where you step—those farm animals, they aren't house-trained, you know."

So, Fred bought a small farm. It had everything a farm needs. It had a barn and sheds, farm equipment and tools. It had lots of animals, a duck pond, and even had a swimming pool.

Fred loaded up Annie and Jennifer and all his belongings, and they moved to their new home.

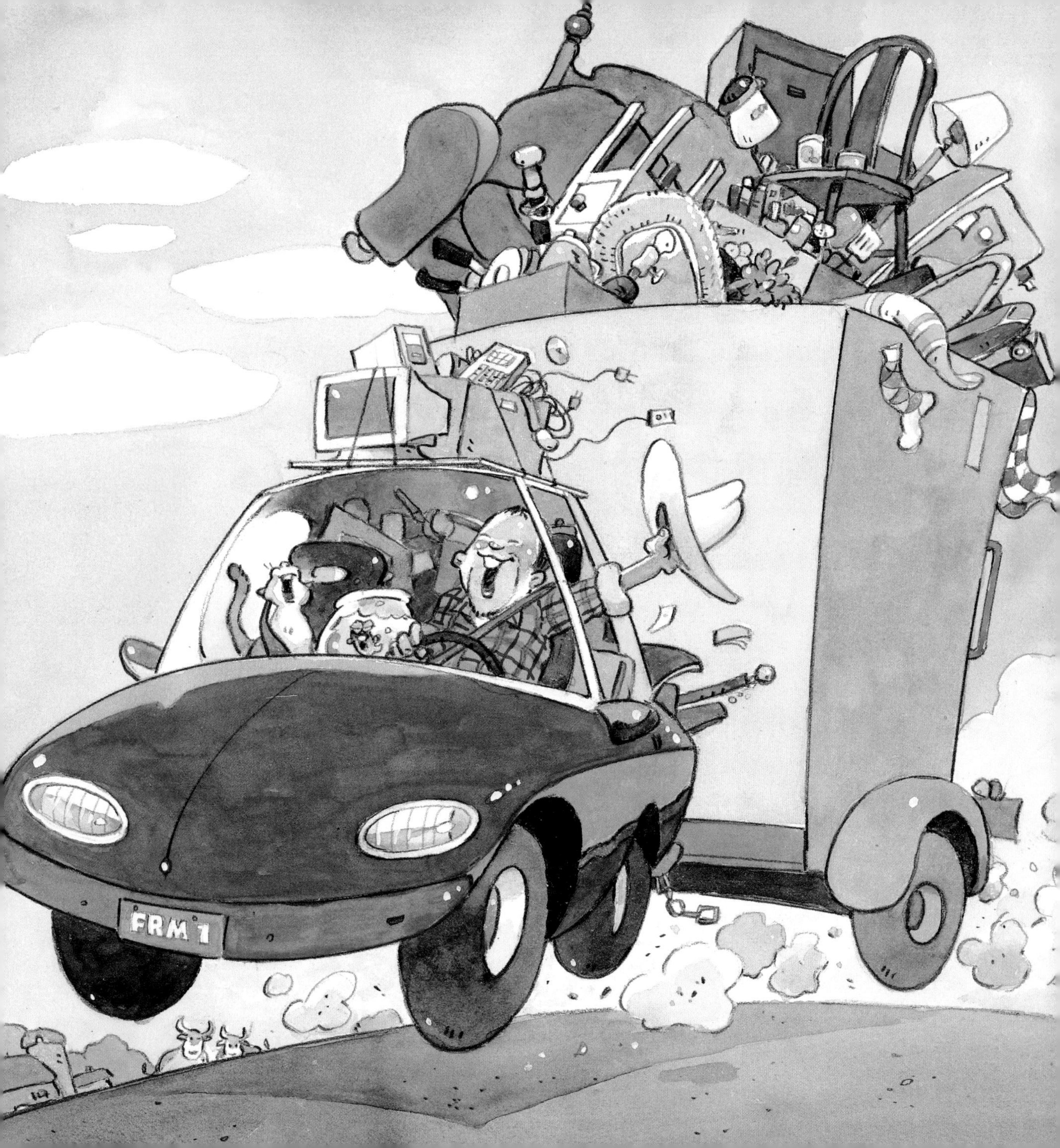
FRM 1

"Wow, this is going to be great," he thought. "I feel better already, and I even think my eyes are getting rounder!"

Next morning, Fred's alarm clock went off. MOOOOO! "Moo?"

Fred sat up. His bedroom was full of animals.

"What the heck are you all doing in here?" shouted Fred. "Out, out. Everybody out! Get outside where you belong."

Fred shooed all the animals out of the house and almost ran over his new neighbor, Mr. Beezuns, and his grandson, Willy.

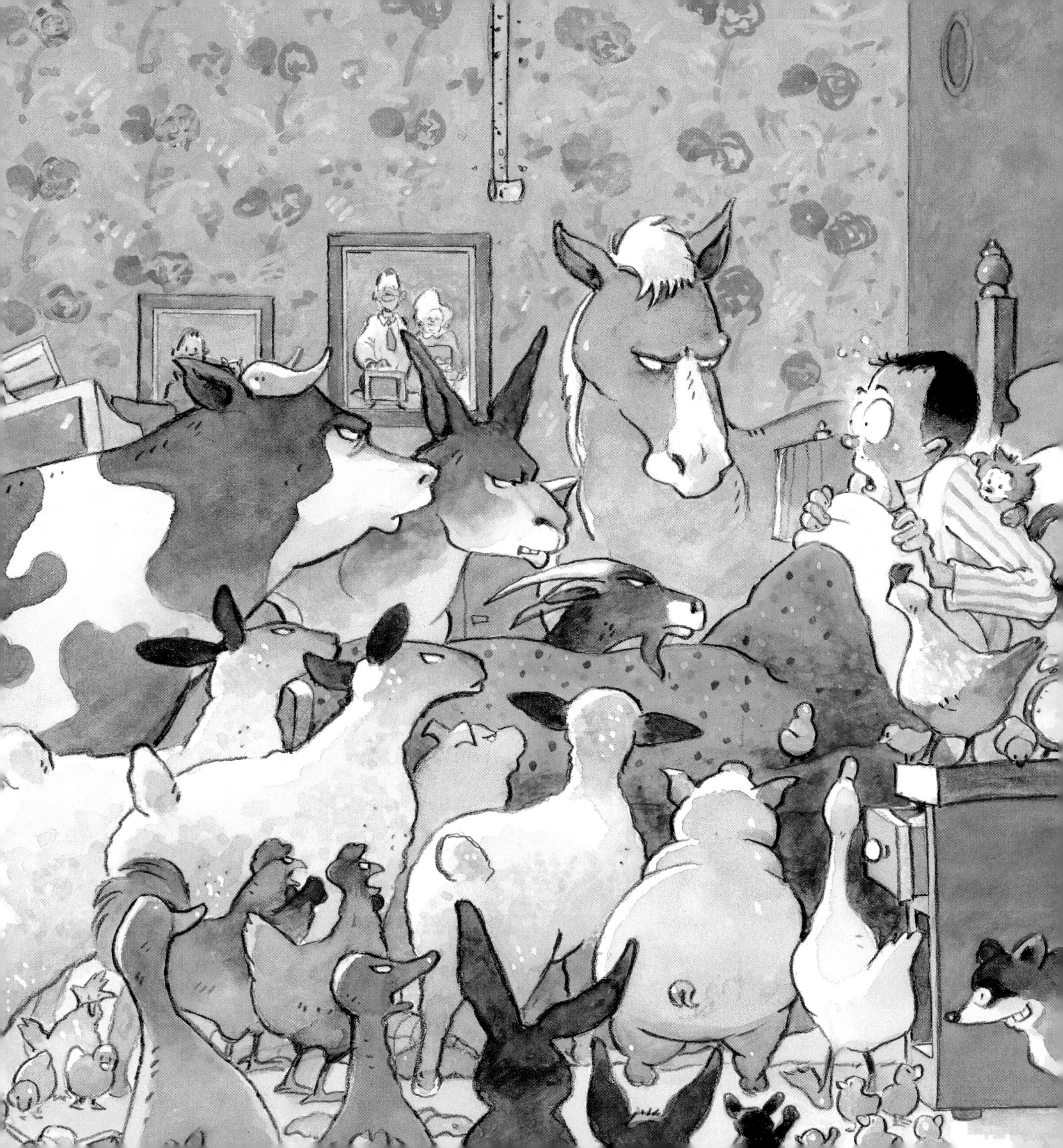

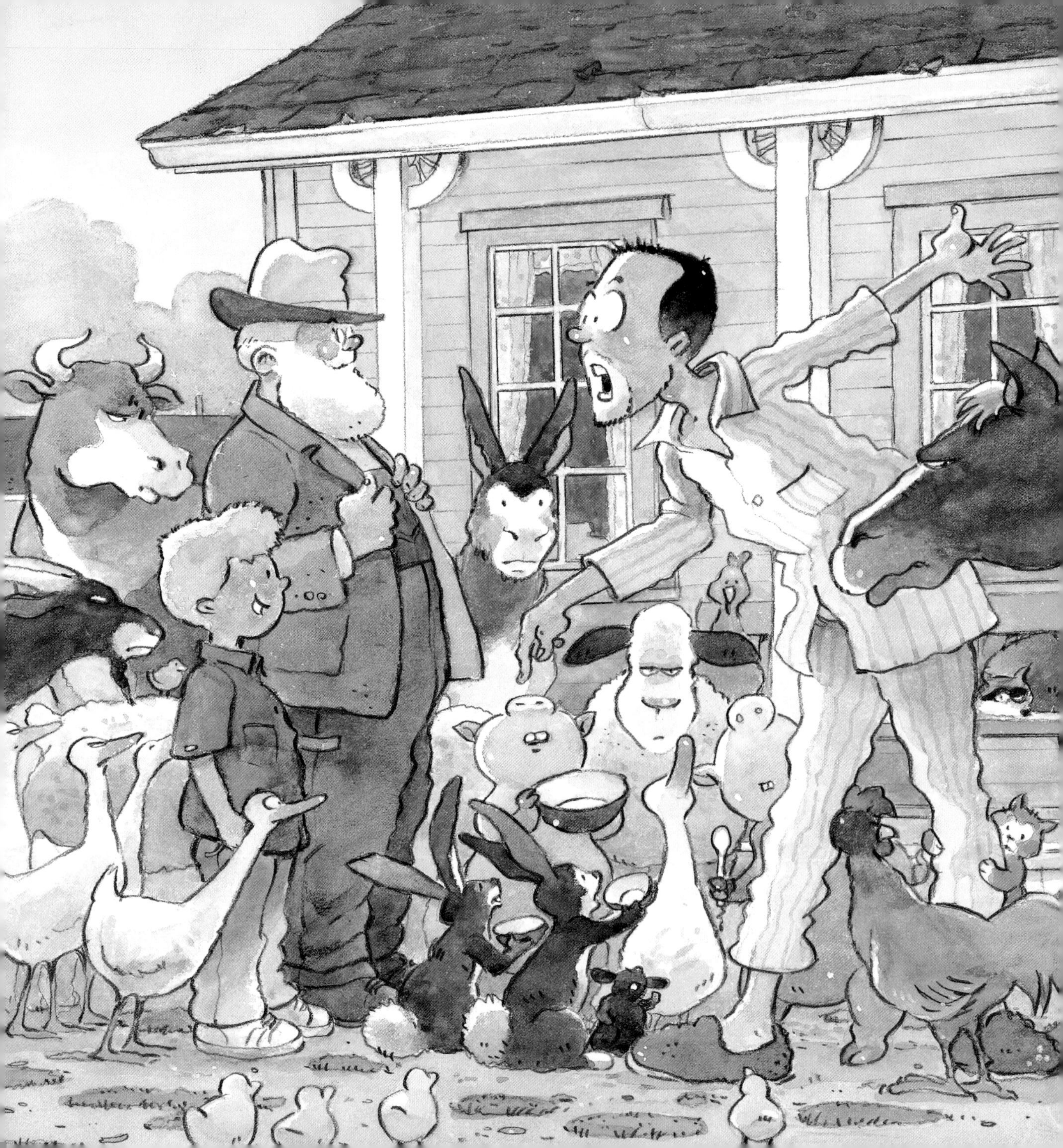

"Having a problem?" asked Mr. Beezuns.

"Well, uh, yes," said Fred. "The animals got into the house and woke me up."

"They're hungry," said Mr. Beezuns.

"It's morning and you've got to feed them," said Willy.

"You didn't go to them, so they came to you," said Mr. Beezuns.

"Feed them!" said Fred. "You mean they don't feed themselves? I thought they just ate grass and stuff."

"No sir," said Mr. Beezuns. "On a farm you feed and water all the animals, clean their stalls, put down fresh straw, milk the cows, collect the eggs, and groom the horses."

"Yep," said Willy. "On a farm you do chores."

"Chores, schmores, I'm not doing any chores," snorted Fred, "especially at five in the morning."

"C'mon," coaxed Mr. Beezuns.

"We'll show you how it's done," said Willy. And they did.

They fed and watered, they milked and they cleaned, and only after they had groomed the horses did they go in for their breakfast.

Fred was exhausted. He thought, "It's only nine o'clock! Man, I can't do this every day."

But Fred did do it. He worked from early morning to late at night day after day.

He couldn't even take the weekend off.

Two weeks later Fred fell into bed and groaned.

"That's it. It's over, I'm done. I don't want to be a farmer any more!"

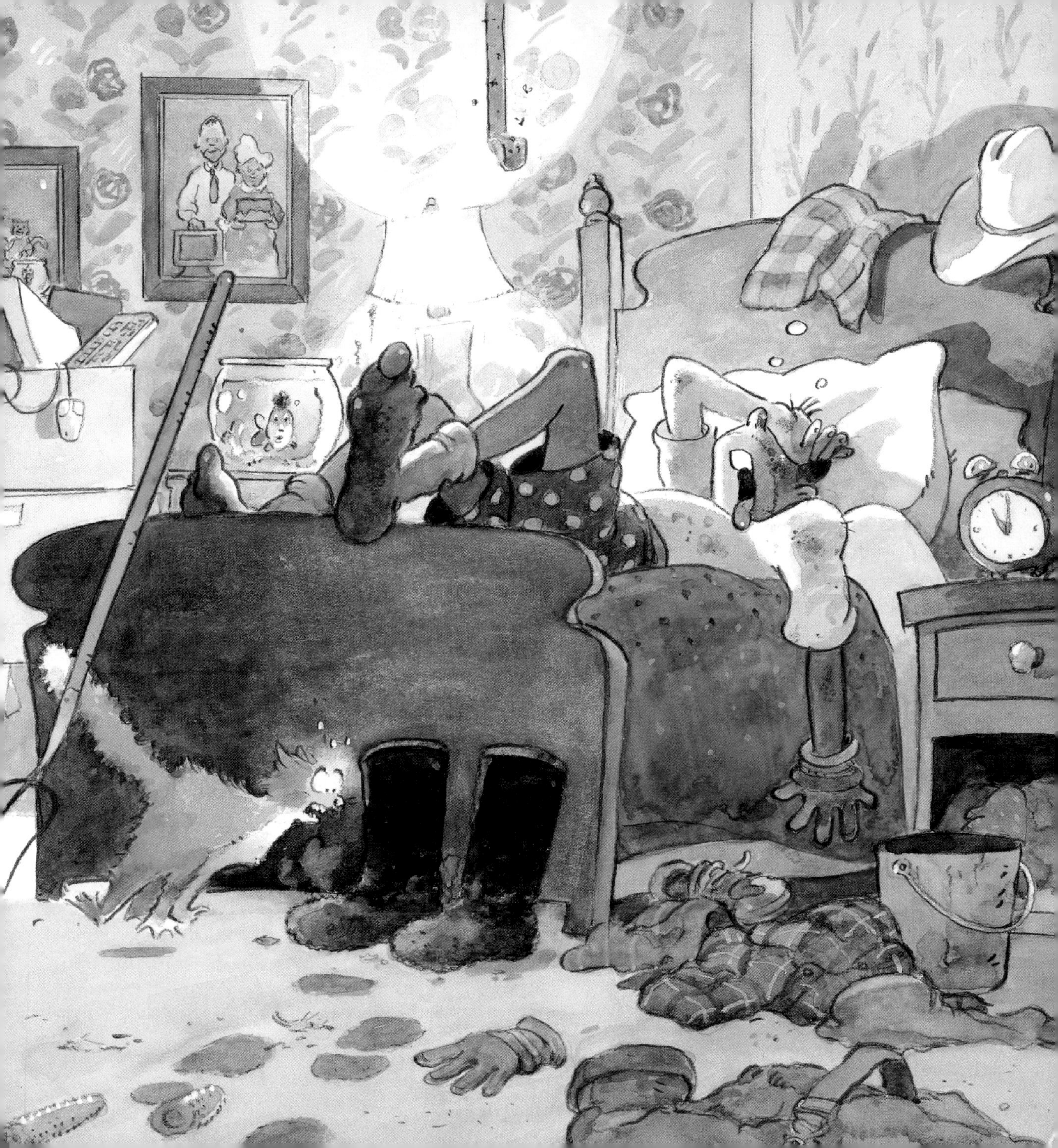

Next morning Willy came by to see how Fred was making out.

"What's up, Fred?" asked Willy.

"I'm quitting," said Fred. "I'm going back to the city. There's just too much work on a farm for one person, and I can't afford to hire anybody."

Willy thought and thought, and then he remembered Fred's computer.

"You don't need to hire anybody, Fred," shouted Willy. "I've got a plan."

Willy explained his plan to Fred. Fred's eyes got bigger as he listened.

"That's brilliant," shouted Fred. "It'll work, let's do it!"

Fred and Willy drove down to the hardware store in the village. They got pipes and wheels, nuts and bolts, connectors and couplings, two boxes of duct tape, and miles and miles of electrical wire.

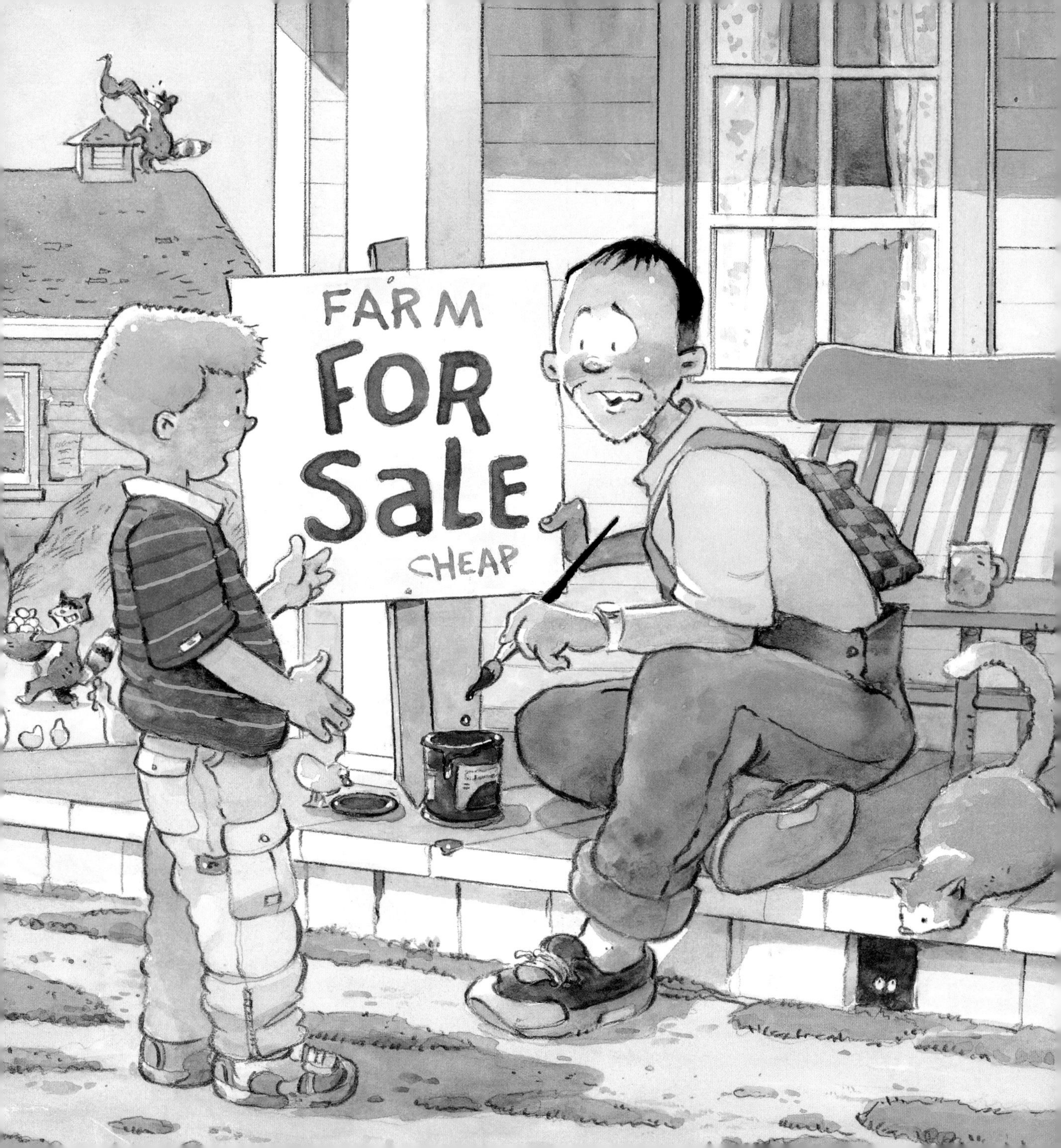
FARM
FOR
SALE
CHEAP

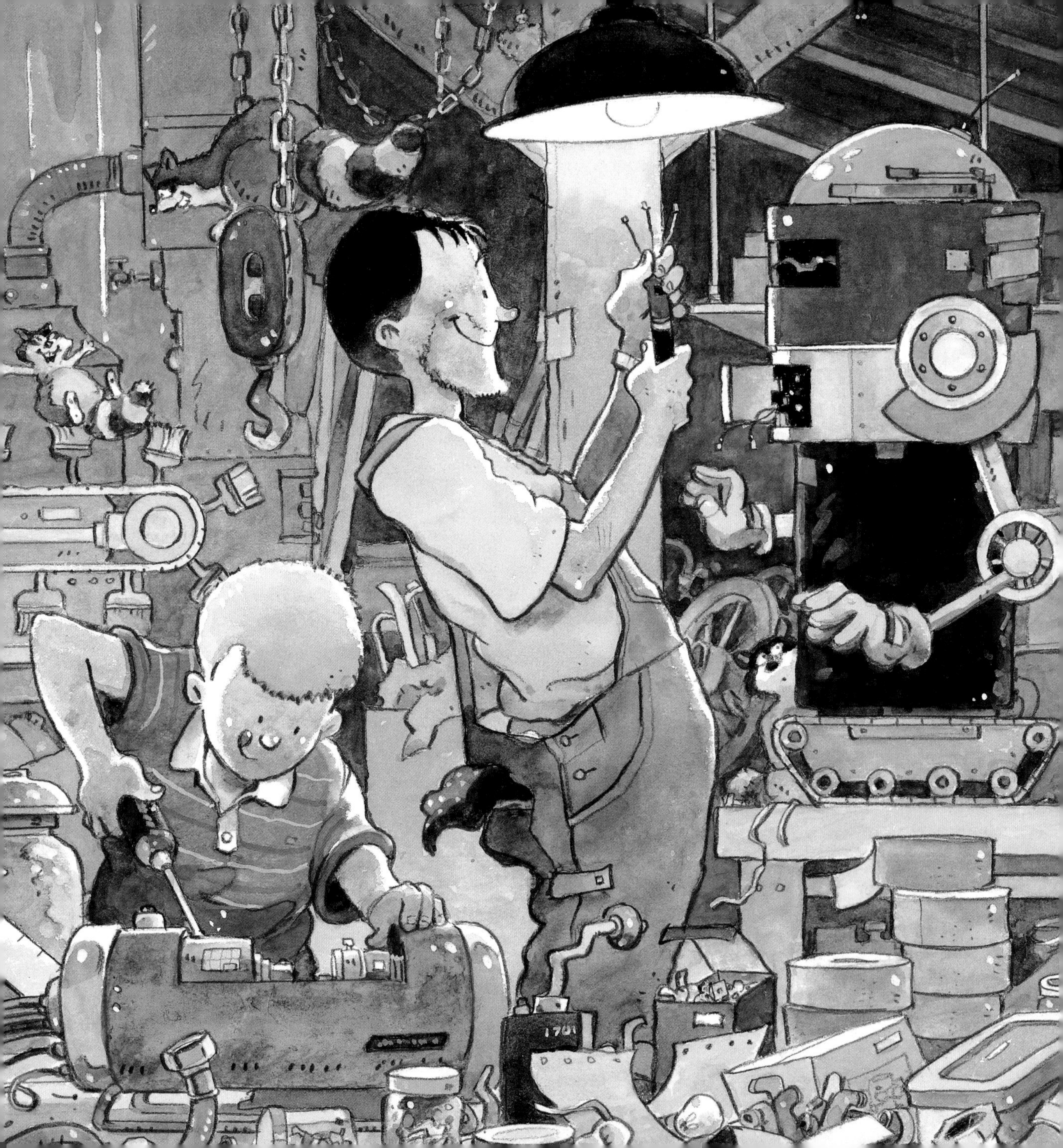

They built an automatic animal feeder and water dispenser. They built an automatic milker, an egg collector, a straw dispenser, and a tractor driver. They built a horse groomer; they even built a pooper scooper.

Then Fred connected everything to his computer.

"This is awesome," said Fred. "I'll just program all these gadgets into this lovely little computer and it will do all the chores! I won't have to get up until noon!"

Fred's gadgets needed power—and lots of it. Big problem! There just wasn't enough power on his little farm.

Fred and Willy scratched their heads, they thought and thought, then Fred got a sly look on his face.

"Ha! I've got it, Willy," he shouted. "Back to the workshop!"

Fred made a huge extension cord. He dragged it down the lane to the large electrical tower and plugged it in.

"Boy, I'm smart," he giggled as he ran back to the house. He flipped on his computer and went outside to watch.

All of Fred's gadgets came to life. The feeder fed, the milker milked, the pooper scooper scooped, and the tractor plowed a beautiful straight furrow on the field.

Everything worked perfectly… for about ten seconds.

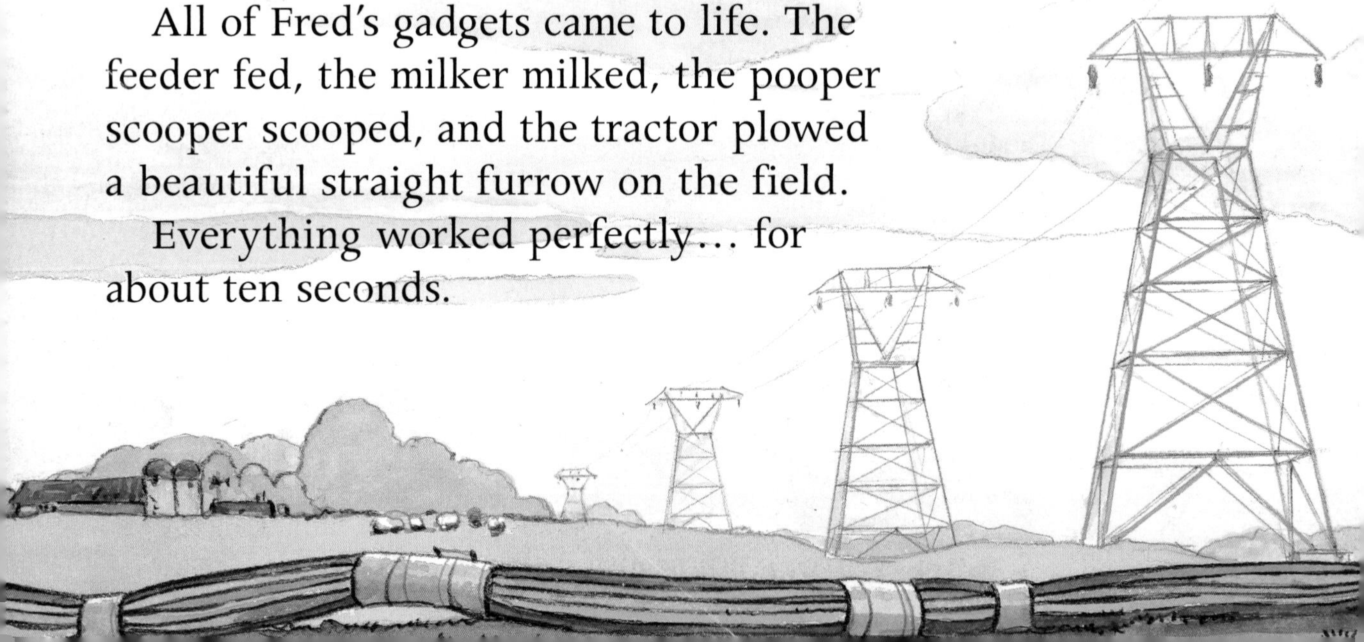

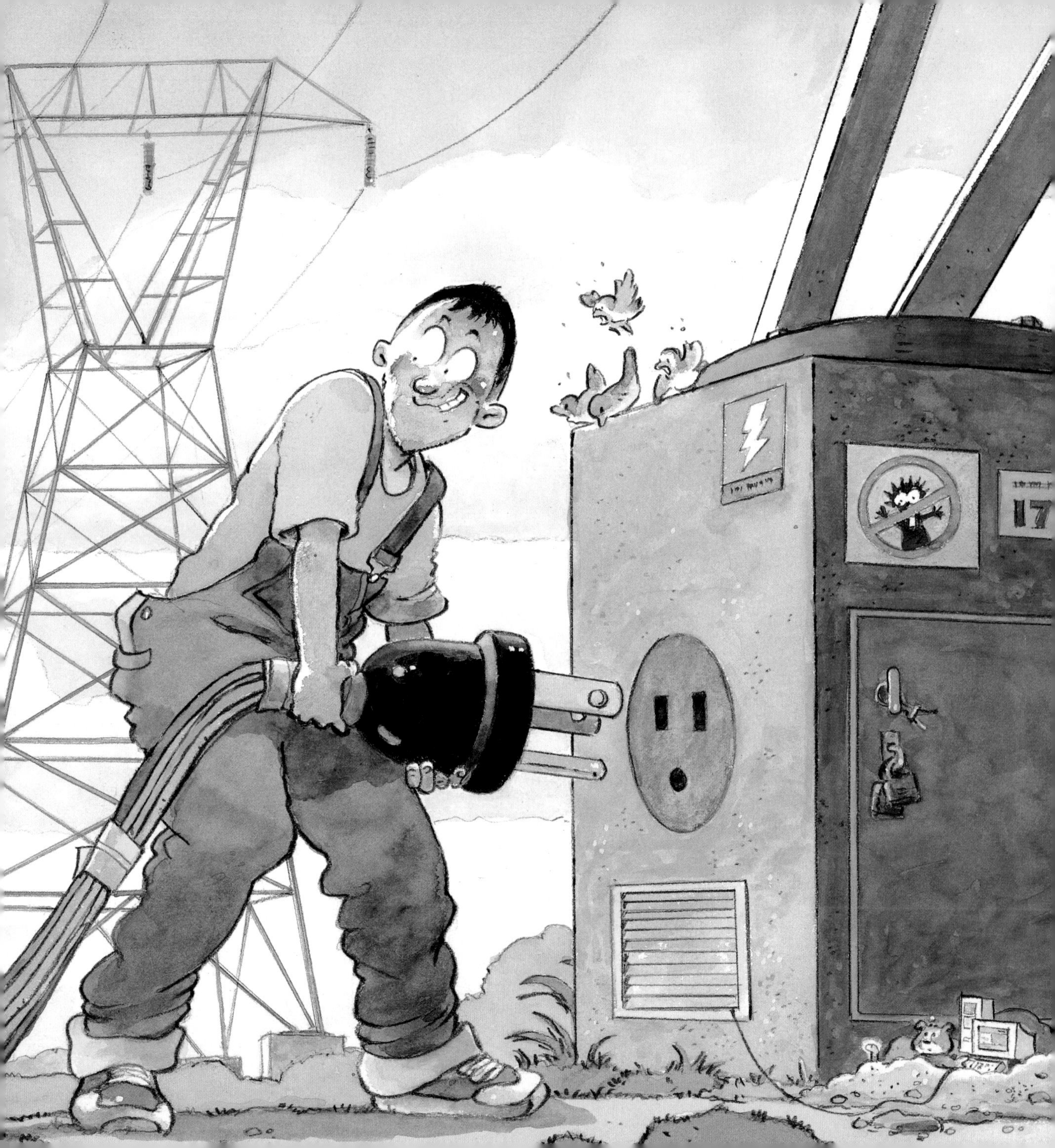
17

Suddenly, there was a loud bang, and a large cloud of gray smoke billowed up, sparks flew from the electrical tower, and power on the farm went off. Then all the power in the village went off, then in the city, and finally the whole country.

Fred ran inside and hid under his bed.

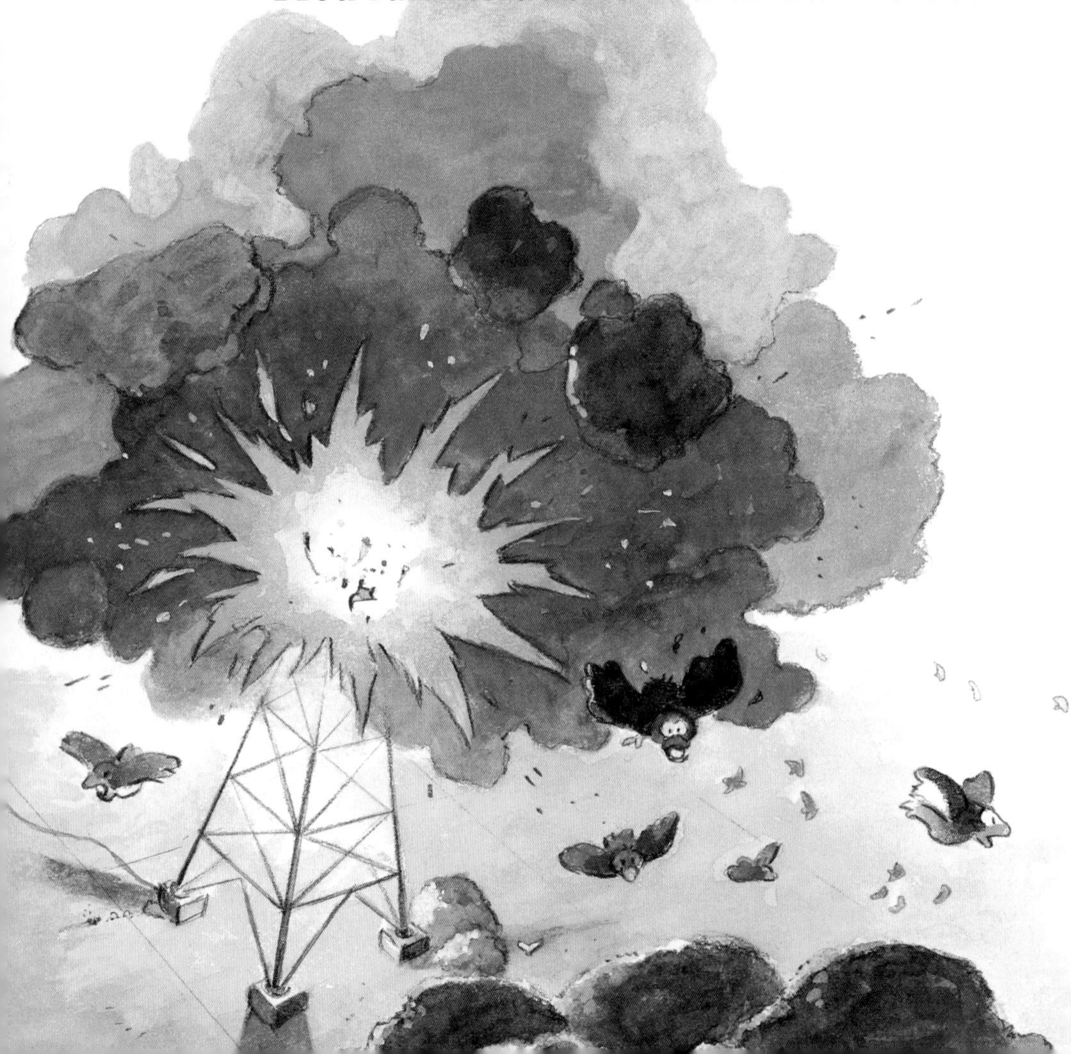

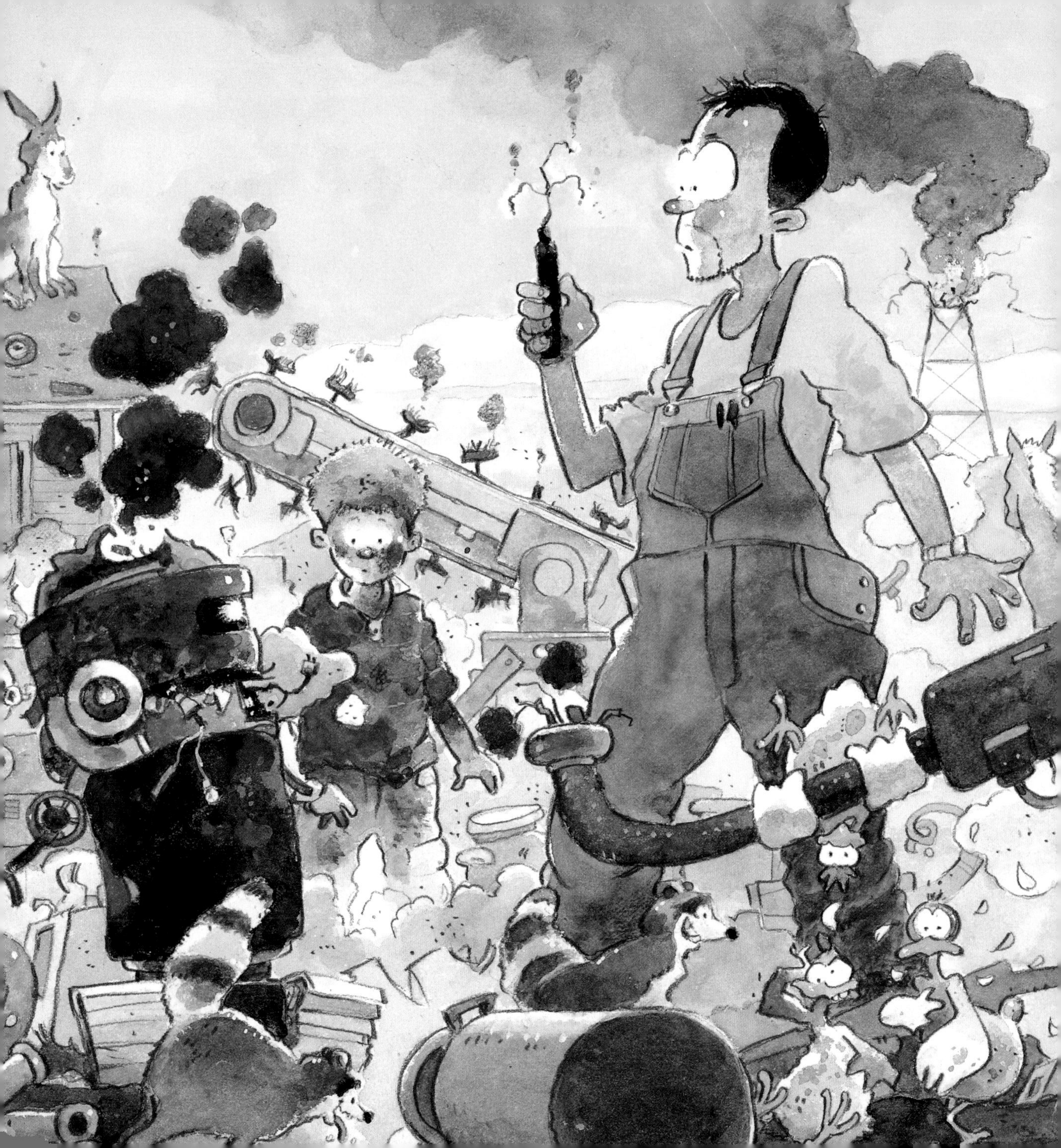

Next morning, when Fred came outside, there were people all over his lawn. They were waving signs. They were really mad.

Even his mother was there.

"Fred," she said, "your blackout made me miss my soaps and ruined my prize-winning cakes."

"Power to the people!" chanted the crowd. "Don't mess with our electricity!"

"You have violated the *Hydro Electric Do Not Be a Power Piggy Act … Section 364B*," growled the man from the electricity company.

"What does that mean?" asked Fred.

"You're cut off for a year!"

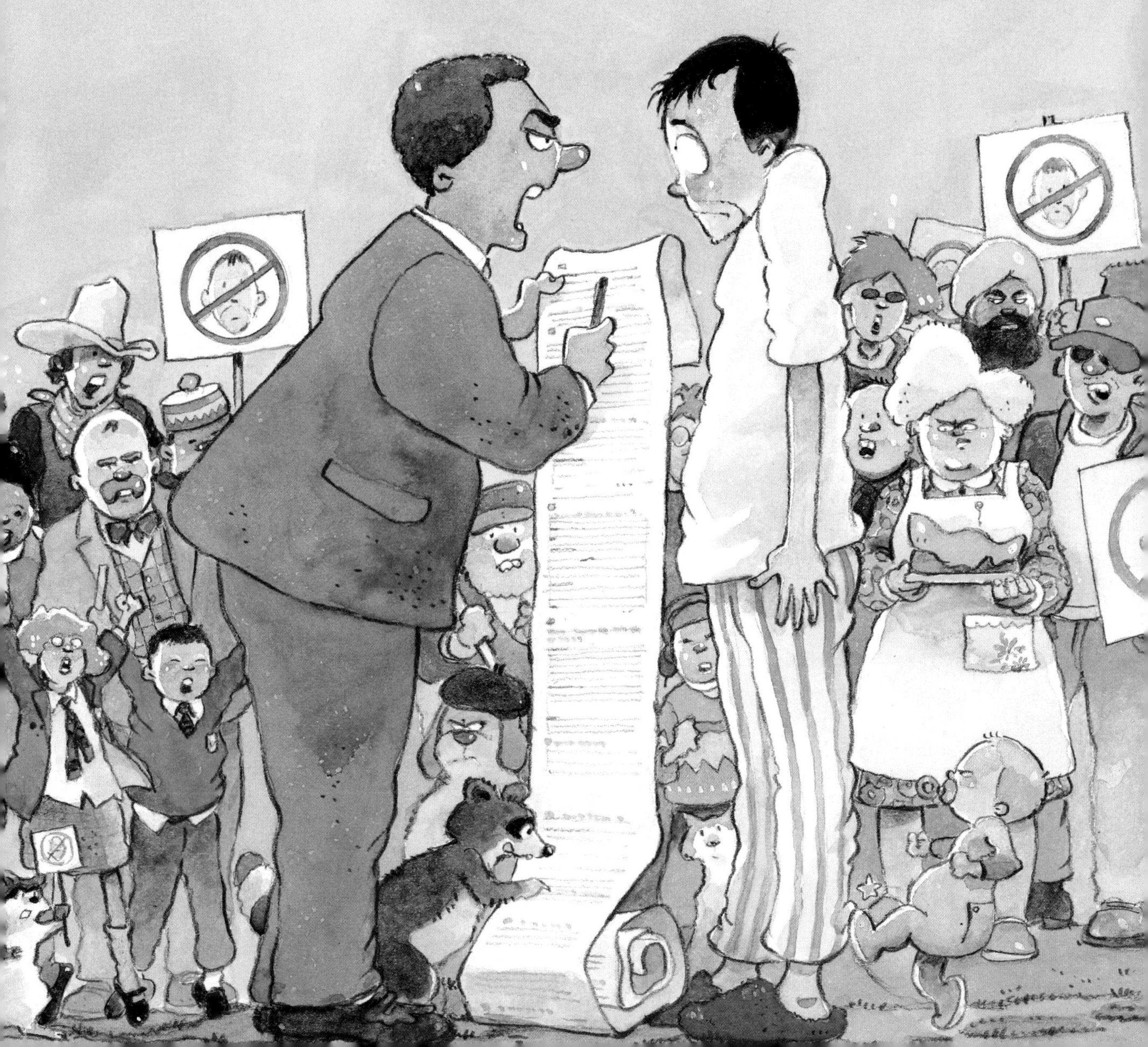

Finally, everyone left and it was quiet again.

Fred sat dejectedly on a bale of hay with Willy and Mr. Beezuns.

"That's great," he said, "now I don't have any electricity at all."

"I still say the old-fashioned ways are the best," said Mr. Beezuns.

"Yeah, maybe," mumbled Fred, "but modern's good, too."

"Sure it is," said Willy, "so why can't you make your own juice?"

"But," said Fred, "I'm broke. How can we do it?"

"Well," said Willy, "there's a lot of great stuff in that old tool shed of yours."

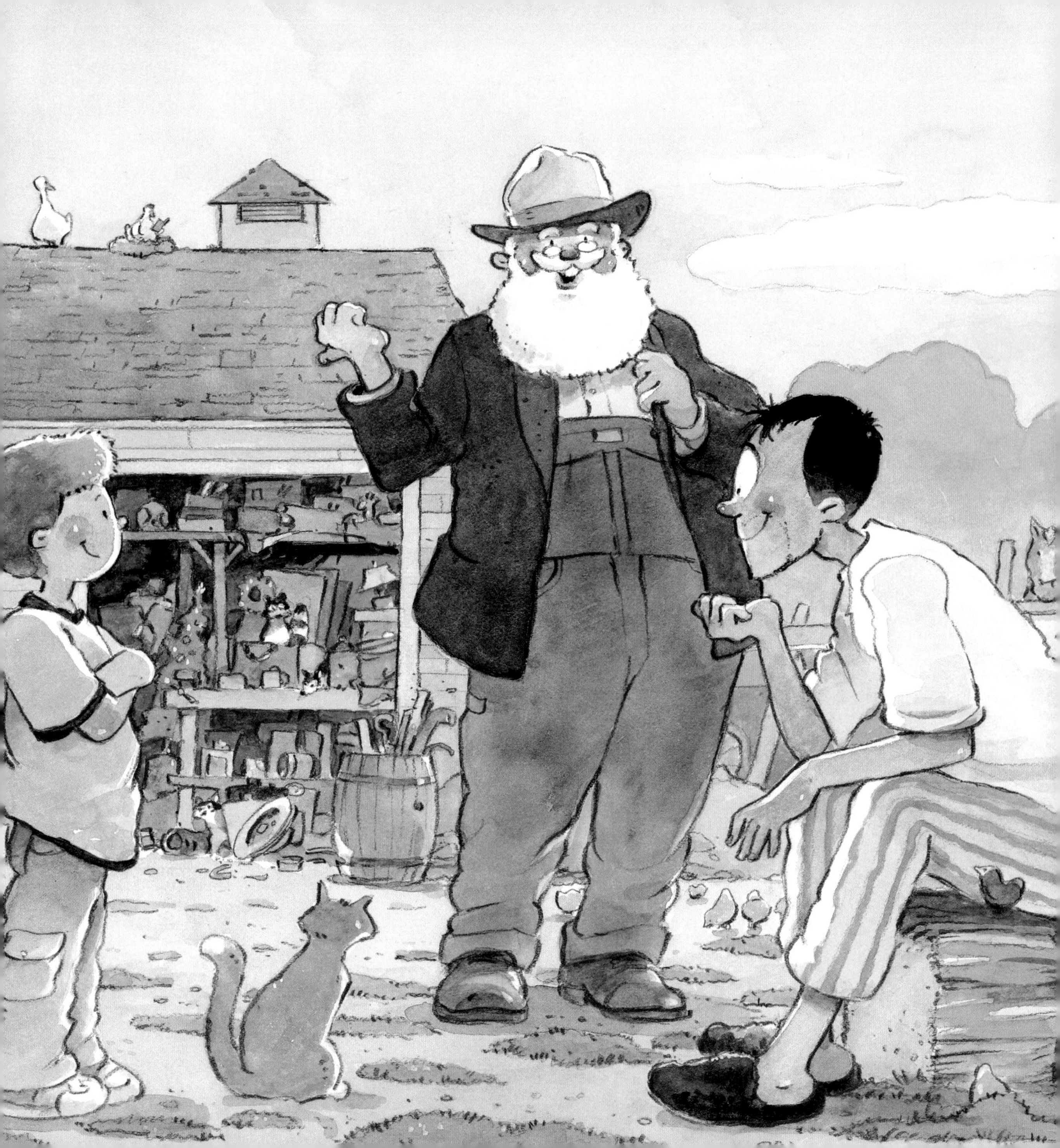

They built solar panels, windmills, and even a big water wheel in the duck pond. When they finished, Fred wrapped all the wires together and connected them to a huge power box. Then he plugged his computer into it. Everything worked perfectly!

When Fred's mom came to visit, he exclaimed, "See, Ma, this is how to be a farmer. Now let me make you some more tea."

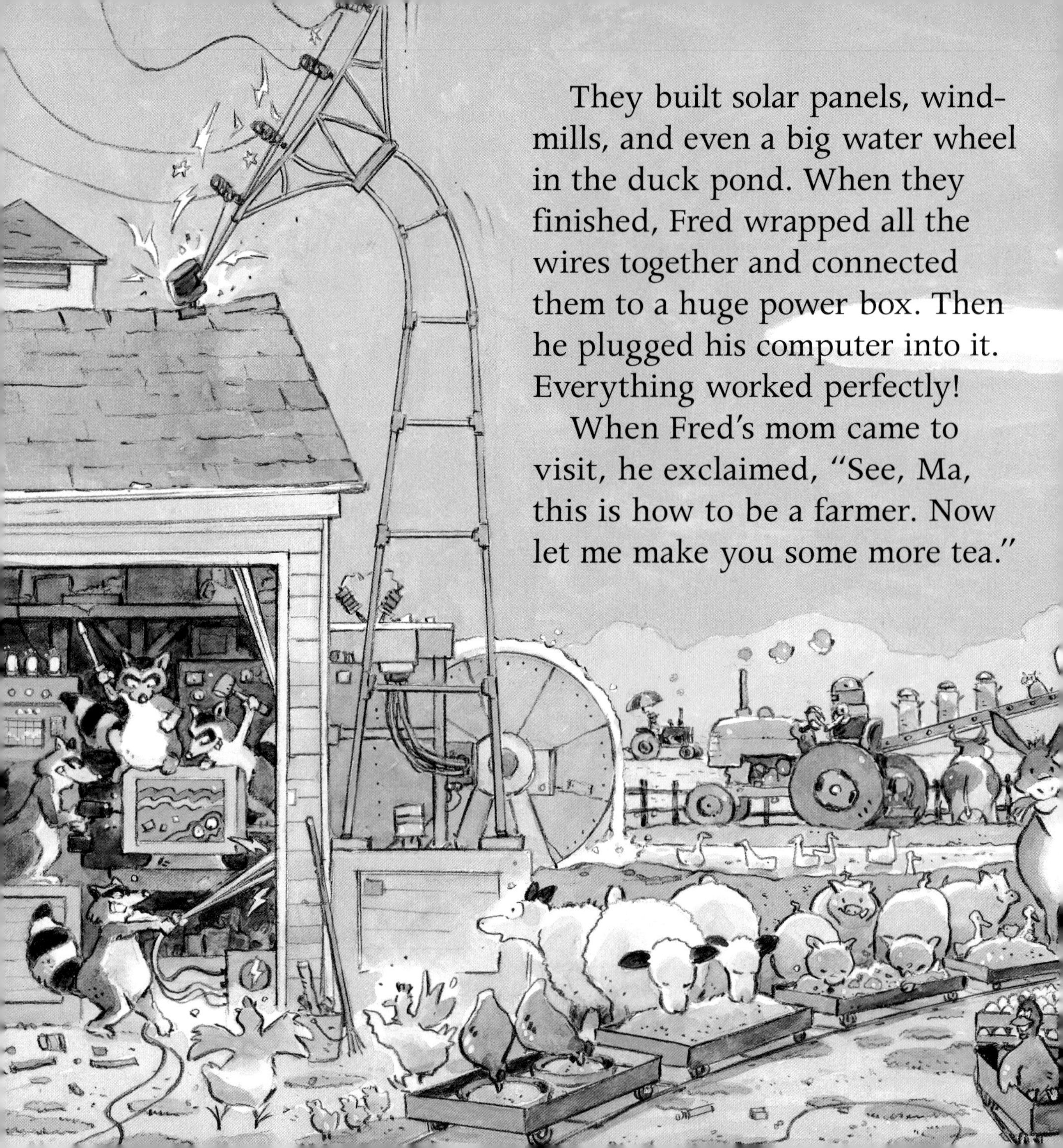

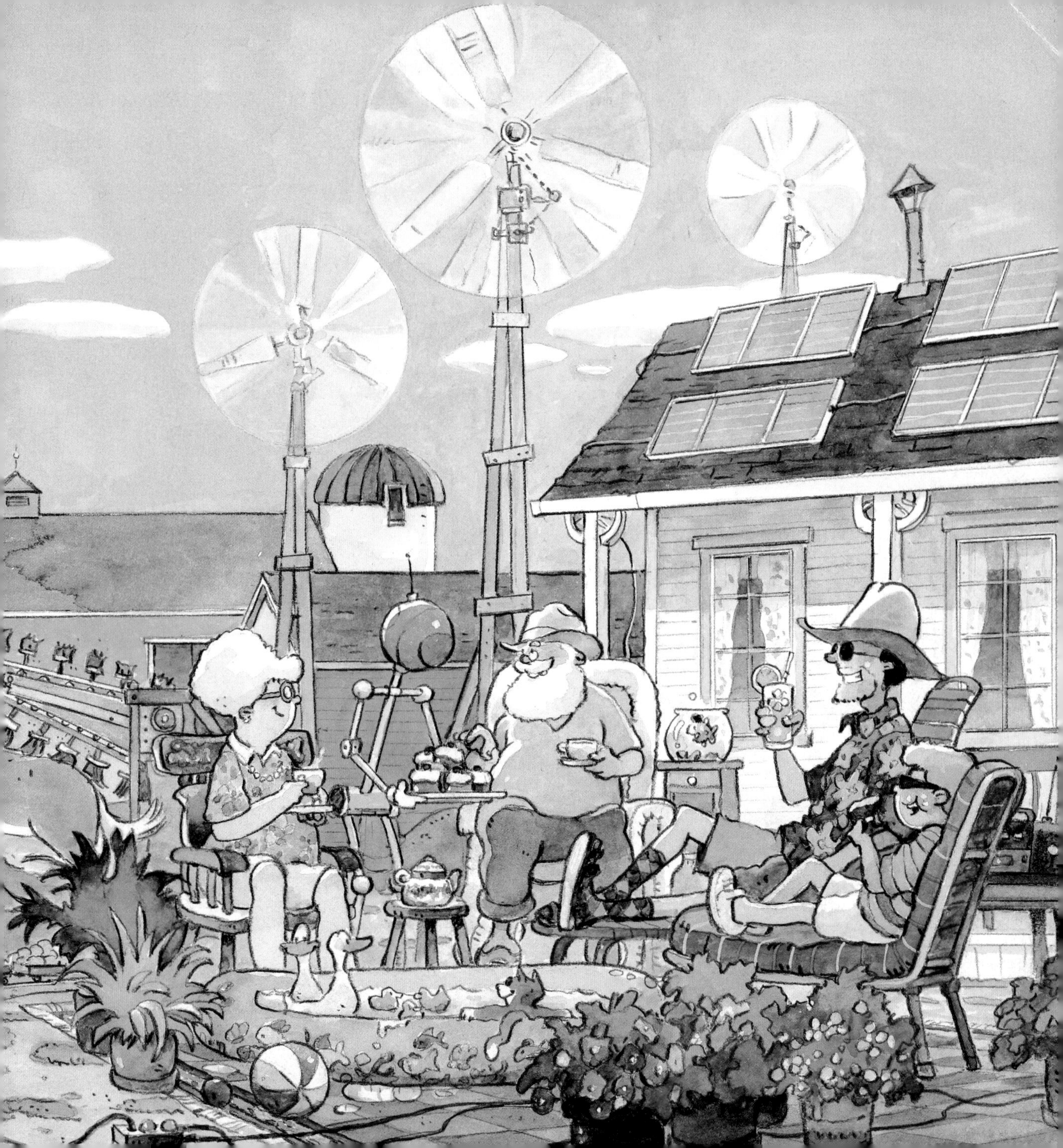

And then Fred plugged in the kettle.

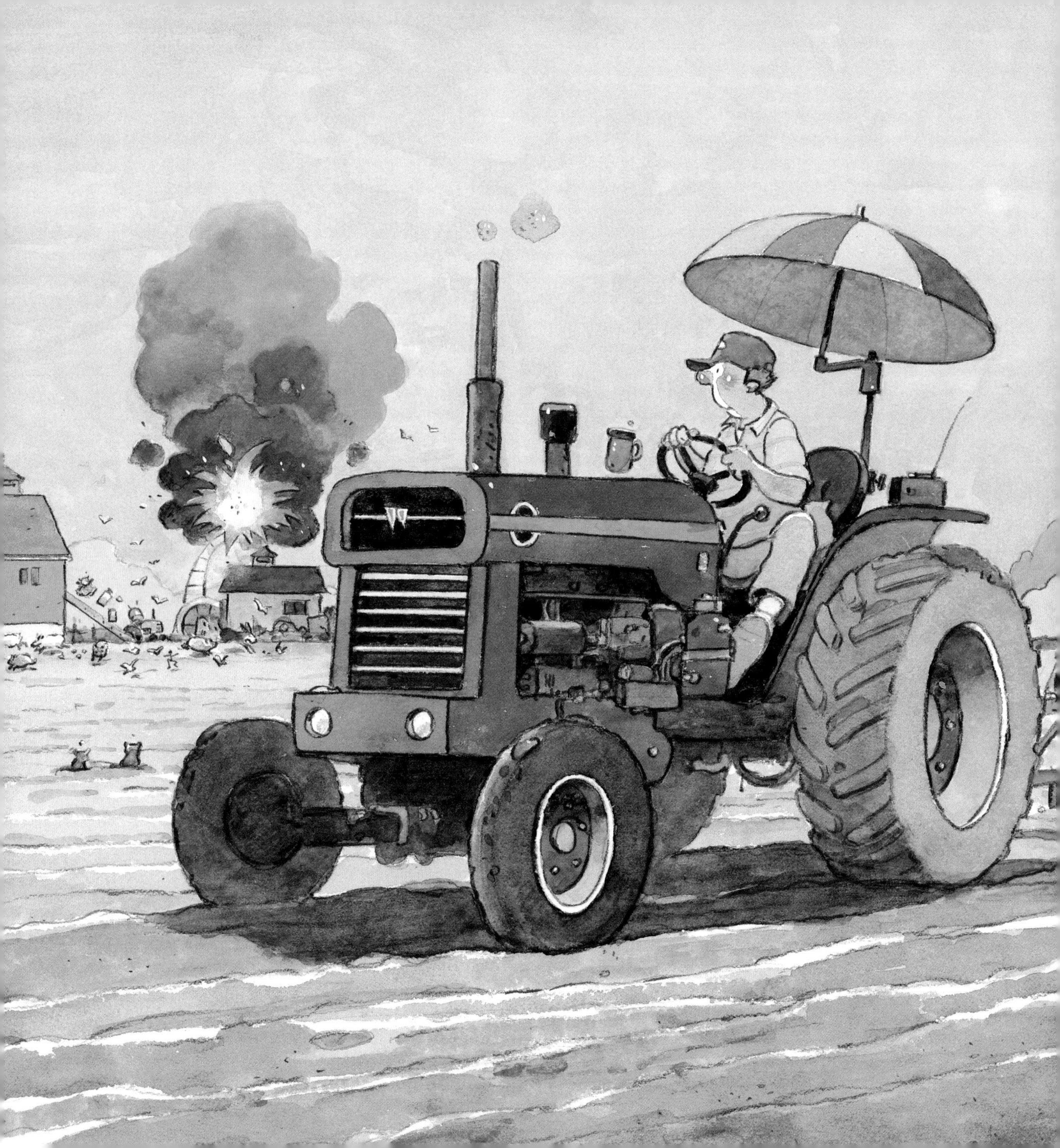

Annick Press Ltd.
All rights reserved. No part of this work covered by the copyrights hereon may
be reproduced or used in any form or by any means – graphic, electronic, or
mechanical – without the prior written permission of the publisher.

We acknowledge the support of the Canada Council for the Arts, the Ontario
Arts Council, the Government of Ontario through the Ontario Book Publishers
Tax Credit program and the Ontario Book Initiative, and the Government of
Canada through the Book Publishing Industry Development Program (BPIDP) for
our publishing activities.

Cataloging in Publication

Martchenko, Michael
        Ma, I'm a farmer / written and illustrated by Michael Martchenko.

ISBN 1-55037-697-7 (bound).--ISBN 1-55037-696-9 (pbk.)

        I. Title.

PS8576.A8593M3 2003   jC813'.54   C2003-901722-2

The art in this book was rendered in watercolor.
The text was typeset in Apollo.

Distributed in Canada by: Published in the U.S.A. by Annick Press (U.S.) Ltd.
Firefly Books Ltd.   Distributed in the U.S.A. by:
3680 Victoria Park Avenue   Firefly Books (U.S.) Inc.
Willowdale, ON   P.O. Box 1338
M2H 3K1   Ellicott Station
                                   Buffalo, NY 14205

Printed and bound in Canada by Friesens, Altona, Manitoba

visit us at: www.annickpress.com